BRER RABBIT

stories

Illustrated by Teresa O'Brien

First published in this edition 1989
Reprinted 1990

Simon & Schuster Young Books
Simon & Schuster Ltd
Wolsey House
Wolsey Road
Hemel Hempstead
Herts HP2 4SS

ISBN 0-7481-0230-2

Printed in Germany

Contents

Brer Rabbit and The Moon

THERE were times when all the creatures became friendly together and shared everything. Then Brer Rabbit forgot his wicked ways, and Brer Fox and Brer Bear, they called on him and all smoked a cigar together.

One time, when they were friends like this, Brer Rabbit saw that he was getting fat and lazy. This always happened when he didn't do any tricks, and the more peace there was, the worse Brer Rabbit felt. And by and by he got very restless.

When the sun shone he'd go and lie in the grass and kick at the gnats, and nibble at the mullein-stalks and wallow in the sand. But this didn't make him any thinner. One night, after supper, whilst he was running round a bit to try and get thinner, he came up with old Brer Terrapin, and after they had shaken hands and sat down on the side of the road, they began to talk about old times.

"You know, Brer Terrapin," said Brer Rabbit, at last, "I just feel I've simply got to have some fun."

"Well, Brer Rabbit," said Brer Terrapin, "then I'm the man for you to have your fun with. What are we going to do?"

"We'll play a trick on Brer Fox, Brer Wolf and Brer Bear," said Brer Rabbit. "We'll all meet down by the mill-pond tomorrow night and have a fishing party. I'll do the talking, and you can say 'yes' to all I say."

Brer Terrapin laughed. "If I'm not there tomorrow night you'll know a grasshopper has run off with me!" he said.

Well, Brer Rabbit set out for home, and on the way he told all the others about the fishing party and they were pleased and promised to be at the mill-pond the next night. Mrs. Meadows and the girls got to hear of the party and they said they'd come along too.

Sure enough, when the time came, they were all there. Brer Bear fetched a hook and line, Brer Fox fetched a dip-net, and Brer Terrapin fetched a box of bait.

Mrs. Meadows and the girls they stood by the edge of the pond and squealed every time Brer Terrapin shook the box of bait at them. Brer Bear said he was going to fish for mudcats. Brer Wolf said he was going to get horny-heads. Brer Fox said he'd catch some perch for the ladies. Brer Terrapin said he wanted to catch minnows and Brer Rabbit winked at Brer Terrapin and said he was after a few silly-billies!

Well, they all got ready, and Brer Rabbit marched up to the pond as if he were going to throw his hook into the water—but just as he was about to fling it in he stopped and stared hard at the water as if he saw something queer there. The other creatures all stopped and watched him. Brer Rabbit dropped his rod and stood scratching his head, looking down into the water.

Mrs. Meadows and the girls felt a bit uncomfortable when they saw Brer Rabbit staring hard like this. "Heyo, Brer Rabbit," they called, "what in the name of goodness is the matter with the water?"

Well, Brer Rabbit went on scratching his head and looking into the

water, and by and by he took a long breath and said: "Folks, we might just as well pack up and go because there won't be any fishing for us!"

With that old Brer Terrapin scrambled to the edge of the water and looked in. He shook his head, and said: "To be sure—to be sure! Tut-tut-tut! That's so, Brer Rabbit, that's surely so!" And then he crawled back again as if he were thinking hard.

"Don't be scared, folks," said Brer Rabbit. "There isn't much the matter except that the moon has dropped into the water! If you don't believe me you can look for yourself."

Well, Brer Fox looked into the pond, and said, "Well, well, well—sure enough, there's the moon!"

Brer Wolf looked in. "Mighty bad, mighty bad!" he said.

Brer Bear looked in and gave a grunt. "Who'd have thought it, who'd have thought it?" he said.

Mrs. Meadows and the girls looked in too and said, "Isn't it too bad!"

Then Brer Rabbit looked in again and said: "Well, folks, it's no good shaking your heads and sighing about it. Unless we get the moon out of the pond there'll be no fish for us to catch tonight! And if you ask Brer Terrapin, he'll tell you the same."

"But how can we get the moon out of the pond?" asked everyone.

"Better leave that to Brer Rabbit," said Brer Terrapin.

Brer Rabbit shut his eyes and looked as if he were thinking deeply. Then by and by he spoke. "The quickest way out of this difficulty is to send to old Mr. Mud Turtle and borrow his drag-net, and drag the moon up from there."

"Well, I'm very glad to hear you say that," said Brer Terrapin, "because old Mr. Mud Turtle is my uncle, and he'll do anything for me."

So Brer Rabbit went for the drag-net, and whilst he was gone old Brer Terrapin began to talk. "You know, folks," he said, "I've heard that those who find the moon in the water and fetch it out find a full pot of money there too! Yes, I've heard that tale time and again!"

This made Brer Fox, Brer Wolf and Brer Bear feel mighty good.

"Seeing that Brer Rabbit has been good enough to go to fetch the drag-net, we'll do the dragging," they said. When Brer Rabbit got back, he saw what was up, and he pretended he was going in after the moon, but the other creatures stopped him.

"You're a dry-foot man," they said to Brer Rabbit. "You don't like the water. We'll do the dragging for the moon."

So Brer Fox, he took hold of one end of the net, Brer Wolf took hold of the other end, and Brer Bear he waded along behind to lift the net up.

They made one haul with the net and lifted it up. No moon! They made another haul—no moon! They dragged the net again—no moon! Then by and by they waded farther out from the bank. Water ran into Brer Fox's ears, and he shook his head. Water ran into Brer Wolf's ears, and he shook his head too. Water ran into Brer Bear's ears, and he had to shake his head as well. And whilst they were all busy shaking their ears, they waded out to a very deep part where the bottom of the pond dropped right away!

Brer Fox stepped off the bottom and went right under! Brer Wolf ducked himself and went under too, and Brer Bear he plunged in and disappeared as well! And goodness gracious, they all kicked and spluttered and splashed as if they wanted to throw all the water out of the mill-pond.

When they came out Mrs. Meadows and the girls were laughing and giggling, and well they might, for Brer Fox, Brer Wolf and Brer Bear looked mighty queer. Brer Rabbit took a look at them, and squealed with laughter too.

"Well, folks," he said at last, "I expect we'd all better go home and get into dry clothes. Better luck next time! I hear that the moon will take a bait of silly-billies, and it seems as if she found her bait all right tonight!"

And with that Brer Rabbit and Brer Terrapin went off to have supper with Mrs. Meadows and the girls, and Brer Fox, Brer Wolf and Brer Bear went off dripping—and what they said about Brer Rabbit that night would have made his ears drop off, if he could have heard!

Brer Rabbit and Brer Bear

ONE SUMMER Brer Fox said to himself that he'd better hurry up and plant his pea-patch. So he got his spade, dug up his ground and planted out his peas.

Old Brer Rabbit came by when he was planting them, and when he thought of juicy ripe peas he winked his eye at his children and sang:

"Ti-yi! Tungalees!
I'll eat his peas, I'll pick his peas!
I'll get each pod and give it a squeeze,
Ti-yi! What juicy peas!"

Sure enough when the peas began to ripen, Brer Fox found that someone had been down in the pea-patch, eating his peas, and he felt mighty mad. He guessed he knew who the someone was, but old Brer Rabbit was so smart that Brer Fox really didn't know how to catch him.

By and by, one day Brer Fox took a walk all round his pea-patch and it wasn't long before he found a hole in the fence that had been rubbed quite smooth with somebody passing in and out.

"Look at that!" said Brer Fox to himself. "Right there is where the thief comes in and out. This is where I'll set a trap!"

He saw a young hickory tree growing nearby. He took a piece of string and tied one end to the top of the tree. He pulled the string and the tree bent half over. Then Brer Fox made a loop-knot at the other end of the string and fixed it neatly round the hole in the fence, keeping it in place with a stick. As soon as anyone crept in through the hole, the string would tighten round him, and the hickory tree would jerk up straight, taking the robber with it, swinging on the end of the string. My, that would be a fine scare for old Brer Rabbit, next time he came lolloping in through the hole!

Next morning, when old Brer Rabbit came slipping along and crept through the hole, the loop-knot caught him tightly, the hickory flew up straight, and there was Brer Rabbit swinging between the earth and sky!

There he swung, afraid of falling, and yet afraid of not falling—for he didn't know what old Brer Fox would say when he came along and found him there!

While he was making up a tale to tell to Brer Fox when he came, he heard a lumbering noise down the road, and presently along came Brer Bear. Brer Rabbit hailed him.

"Heyo, Brer Bear!"

Brer Bear looked about in surprise, and by and by he saw Brer Rabbit swinging from the tree.

"Heyo, Brer Rabbit!" he shouted. "How are you this morning?"

"Much obliged to you, I'm just middling," said Brer Rabbit.

"What are you doing up there?" asked Brer Bear in surprise.

"Huh, I'm making a shilling a minute up here," said Brer Rabbit.

"How's that?" asked Brer Bear, still more surprised.

"I'm up here frightening the crows out of Brer Fox's pea-patch," said Brer Rabbit. "Brer Fox pays me well for it."

"That's a fine job," said Brer Bear.

"Well, you come and have a turn at it," said Brer Rabbit, in a generous sort of voice. "You've a large family of children to work for, Brer Bear, and you'd make a fine scarecrow. I don't mind letting you have my job for a little while, just to do you a kindness."

"I'll take it, then," said Brer Bear, pleased. "How do I get up there, Brer Rabbit?"

"Bend down the tree," said Brer Rabbit. "And undo the string. It's quite easy."

Well, it wasn't long before Brer Rabbit was safely on the ground and old Brer Bear was swinging high up in Brer Rabbit's place. Then Brer

Rabbit he set out for Brer Fox's house, shouting:

"Brer Fox! Oh, Brer Fox! Come out here Brer Fox, and I'll show you the man who's been stealing your peas!"

Brer Fox grabbed his walking-stick, and went running down to his pea-patch. When he got there, sure enough there was old Brer Bear swinging in the trap!

"Oh yes! You're caught!" said Brer Fox, and before Brer Bear could explain, Brer Rabbit jumped up and down shouting:

"Yes, there's the robber, Brer Fox! Whip him well, and don't you listen to any cheek from him!"

So, every time poor Brer Bear tried to explain how he came to be there, Brer Fox hit him a whack with his walking-stick, and made him squeal so that he couldn't say a word.

Whilst all this was going on, Brer Rabbit slipped off and got deep down into a mud-hole, for he knew Brer Bear would be after him as soon as he was free. He just left his big eyes sticking out of the mud-hole, for all the world like a frog peeping out.

By and by old Brer Bear came galloping down the road, looking everywhere for Brer Rabbit. When he got to the mud-hole he saw Brer Rabbit's eyes sticking out.

"Howdy, Brer Frog!" he said. "Have you seen Brer Rabbit?"

"He's just gone by," said Brer Rabbit, and Old Brer Bear shot off down the road like a runaway horse, trying to catch up with Brer Rabbit.

And soon Brer Rabbit came out of the mud-hole, dried himself in the sun, brushed off the mud and went ambling home, whistling a tune he knew:

"*Ti-yi! Tungalees!*
I ate those peas, I picked those peas!
I got each pod and gave it a squeeze,
Ti-yi! What juicy peas!"

Oh, wicked Brer Rabbit!

Brer Rabbit tricks Mr. Lion

Now, one day Mr. Lion came to live mighty near Brer Fox, Brer Wolf, Brer Bear and Brer Racoon.

They didn't like it.

"He roars so loud," said Brer Fox.

"He looks very hungry," said Brer Racoon.

"If Mr. Man comes hunting him, he'll hunt us, too," said Brer Bear.

"Let's get him away," said Brer Wolf.

But nobody knew how to. Mr. Lion built himself a strong house, put in the windows and set in the door.

"It looks as if he's come to stay," said Brer Wolf.

"He bellowed at me yesterday, and gave me such a fright that half my whiskers fell off," said Brer Bear.

"You never had many," said Brer Fox.

"Now, now—don't let's quarrel among ourselves," said Brer Racoon. "If we can't think of anything to make Mr. Lion go, we'd best go to old Brer Rabbit and get his help. He's a mighty clever one, he is."

"Too clever," said Brer Fox, thinking of all the tricks that Brer Rabbit had played on him.

"He couldn't get the better of Mr. Lion," said Brer Wolf. "Mr. Lion is clever, too—and mighty strong. He wouldn't go away for Brer Rabbit."

But in the end the animals had to go and ask Brer Rabbit to help them.

Brer Rabbit was in his house—and a very tumble-down house it was, too! A chimney had fallen off, one of the windows was broken, and the door wouldn't shut properly.

Brer Rabbit saw them coming and leaned out of the window. "What do you want?" he said. "So many friends all at once means something!"

"Brer Rabbit, we want your help," said Brer Wolf. "We don't like Mr. Lion living so near to us. But he won't go. We want you to set your brains to work, and get him away for us."

"Easy!" said Brer Rabbit. "What will you give me if I do?"

"Anything you like," said Brer Bear. "What do you want?"

"Well, I want my house mended up nicely," said Brer Rabbit. "I want a new chimney—and a new window—and a new door—and maybe a new gate, too."

"You shall have them all if you can make Mr. Lion go away," said Brer Bear. "But he's mighty strong, Brer Rabbit, oh, mighty strong! You can't fight *him*, you know."

"Oh, I'll get my friend Brer Terrapin to challenge Mr. Lion," said Brer Rabbit. "I wouldn't bother with him myself. But old Brer Terrapin, he'll do it for me."

The creatures stared at Brer Rabbit. Brer Terrapin was a little thing. How could he do anything against Mr. Lion?

Brer Rabbit got busy soon after that. He went to see Brer Terrapin, and the two of them laughed and chuckled away as they laid their plans.

"Now you know what you've got to do, don't you?" said Brer Rabbit at last. "Here's the rope—see? You do your part and I'll do mine. Now, you go and find Mr. Lion."

Brer Terrapin hurried off to find Mr. Lion. Brer Bear, Brer Wolf, Brer Fox and Brer Racoon saw him going to Mr. Lion's new house, and they followed him, wondering what he was going to do.

Brer Terrapin knocked at Mr. Lion's door.

"Who's there?" bellowed Mr. Lion, and at once everyone but Brer Terrapin went and hid themselves in the bushes.

"It's me, old Brer Terrapin," said Brer Terrapin. "Mr. Lion, Brer Rabbit has sent me to you to say if you don't go away he'll hit you so hard you'll go flying into the middle of next week and never come back!"

Mr. Lion gave such a snort that the door flew open and hit Brer Terrapin on the shell. But Brer Terrapin wasn't a bit frightened!

"You be careful I don't gobble you up, shell and all!" roared Mr. Lion.

"Oh, Mr. Lion, you're not strong enough to do that!" said Brer Terrapin. "No, you're not! Why, if you and I had a rope between us, you at one end and me at the other, I could pull you right over, so I could!"

Mr. Lion roared angrily again, and the door blew shut. "You go and get your rope, and I'll show you how to pull!" he bellowed. "I'll pull you higher than the roof!"

"I'll go and get a rope," said Brer Terrapin, hurrying off. "Will you come to the field, Mr. Lion, where everyone can watch, please?"

Brer Terrapin fetched a very strong rope. Mr. Lion came to the little field and stood there, lashing his tail angrily. Brer Bear, Brer Wolf, Brer

Fox and Brer Racoon crept out of the bushes to watch.

"Now you take this end and stand over there," said Brer Terrapin, and he gave Mr. Lion one end and showed him where to stand. "And I'll take this end of the rope and stand over here by the fence. Let me have a bit of time to get ready. Brer Bear can shout 'pull' in a minute!"

Now, the rope was a very long one. Brer Terrapin took hold of it

24

halfway along. Brer Rabbit was waiting in the bushes, and he picked up the end and ran off with it. He went to Mr. Lion's house nearby, and tied the rope all round it, walls and all. Then he gave a gentle tug, which Brer Terrapin felt. Then Brer Terrapin knew that everything was ready.

"I'm ready, Brer Bear," he yelled. Brer Terrapin was hidden in the long grass by the fence, and all that could be seen of him was the top of his shell. Everyone thought he had the rope in his mouth, ready to pull. But he hadn't. The rope ran through a hole in the fence, right to Mr. Lion's house!

"PULL!" yelled Brer Bear.

And Mr. Lion pulled! At first he didn't pull very hard, for he felt certain that he could pull old Brer Terrapin right off his feet at once. But he wasn't pulling Brer Terrapin. He was pulling his own house! And his house was big and strong.

"Pull, Mr. Lion, pull!" cried Brer Bear, surprised that Mr. Lion couldn't pull Brer Terrapin out of the long grass at once.

"Pull, Mr. Lion, pull!" squealed Brer Terrapin. "You haven't got much strength, Mr. Lion!"

Mr. Lion gave a great bellow and pulled with all his mighty power. And something happened.

He pulled his own house down! There came a tremendous noise of smashing and crashing, of clattering and battering—and down came Mr. Lion's house in a hurry!

Everyone stood listening in amazement—and then they rushed to see what the noise was about.

They jumped over the fence and saw that Mr. Lion's house was in ruins! There it lay on the ground, all fallen to pieces—and there was old Brer Rabbit, kicking the bricks about and pretending to push the bits here and there.

"Brer Rabbit! Hi, Brer Rabbit! Did you push Mr. Lion's house down?" yelled Brer Bear, hardly able to believe his eyes.

"Brer Rabbit! How did you manage to pull that house down?" shouted Brer Fox in amazement.

"Oh, it was quite easy," said Brer Rabbit. "I'm always telling you how strong I am, but you won't believe it. I didn't want to bother to tug against Mr. Lion. I guessed Brer Terrapin could do that all right."

Mr. Lion stared at his ruined house and trembled. Brer Rabbit kicked a brick at him.

"Like to fight me, Mr. Lion?" he asked. "Maybe you feel angry at having your house pushed down, such a strong and fine one it was!"

But Mr. Lion didn't want to fight anyone who could push a house down with a crash and a smash like that! Oh, no! He knew better than that! He put his tail down and slunk off into the woods, a very puzzled and astonished lion indeed.

Brer Bear, Brer Racoon, Brer Wolf and Brer Fox stared in amazement at Brer Rabbit. Brer Terrapin came ambling up.

"What did you want to push Mr. Lion's house down for, just when I was winning the tug-of-war?" he said, pretending to be cross. "I was just about to pull him off his feet, so I was!"

Brer Rabbit turned to Brer Bear and the others. "I want my own house mended quickly," he said, in a very haughty voice. "Brer Bear, take this door of Mr. Lion's and put it into my house for me."

"Yes, sir," said Brer Bear and went off with the door.

"Brer Wolf, put these new windows into my house," ordered Brer Rabbit. "Quick now, or I'll give you a spank."

"Yes sir," said Brer Wolf, humbly.

"And you, Brer Racoon, take this chimney-pot—and you, Brer Fox, take that garden gate and put it into my gate-posts," said Brer Rabbit.

"Yes, sir," said Brer Racoon and Brer Fox.

Off they all went, and Brer Rabbit and Brer Terrapin followed behind, laughing fit to kill themselves.

But not one of the others guessed why. Oh, no—all they said to one another was: "Brer Rabbit's a mighty strong fellow, so he is! Brer Rabbit's a mighty strong fellow! One push, and Mr. Lion's house fell down!"

Brer Fox Goes to Market

ONCE Brer Fox and Brer Rabbit very badly wanted some money, and they tried to plan how to get some.

"We could go and dig in Mr. Man's field and earn some," said Brer Rabbit with a grin.

"Pooh!" said Brer Fox. "That's too much like hard work! Think again, Brer Rabbit, think again!"

"Well, we could find a bee-tree, collect the honey, and take it to market," said Brer Rabbit.

"And get stung all over," said Brer Fox. "You are not very bright today, Brer Rabbit."

"Well, you take a turn at thinking, then," said Brer Rabbit crossly. "I'm getting a headache with thinking so much."

"I've got a fine idea," said Brer Fox. "What about going along to Brer Bear's house and taking a few things to sell at the market?"

"But that's stealing," said Brer Rabbit, quite shocked.

"Well, it would do Brer Bear good to lose a few of his things," said Brer Fox. "But if you think it would be stealing from him, what about going to Miss Goose's house and taking a few of *her* things? She's got some nice sheets and towels we could sell at the market."

"But that would be stealing too," said Brer Rabbit.

"Now if you're going to call everything stealing, I shall stop thinking of

30

plans," said Brer Fox, and he showed his teeth.

"All right, all right," said Brer Rabbit in a hurry. "We'll have your plan. But who does the taking? I don't want to."

"Of course you'll have to," said Brer Fox. "I'll do the selling—and you must do the taking."

"Well does it matter whose house I go to?" asked Brer Rabbit.

"Not a bit," said Brer Fox. "Go to anyone's you like."

"And you are quite sure it won't be stealing?" asked Brer Rabbit.

"Quite, quite sure," said Brer Fox. "Now see you get into someone's house, choose a few things, bring them to me here—and I'll go to market with them. I'll sell them, and you shall have half the money."

"Thank you kindly," said Brer Rabbit. "I'll go straight away, Brer Fox. But mind you stay here till I come back, so that I will know where to find you!"

"I'll stay all right," said Brer Fox with a grin. "Hurry now."

Brer Rabbit hurried off, grinning away to himself. He didn't go to Brer Bear's. He didn't go to Miss Goose's. No—he went to Brer Fox's own house. It was quite empty, of course. Brer Rabbit pushed open the door and looked around.

He took all the spoons and forks out of the drawer. He took all the clean white towels out of the cupboard. He took six pots of jam from the larder. He took a brand new kettle from the stove. That was enough for him to carry, so he hurried back with all his goods to where Brer Fox was waiting impatiently.

"Good!" said Brer Fox, taking all the things. "Now I'll be off to the market to sell all these for as good a price as I can get."

"You are quite, quite sure it wasn't stealing?" said Brer Rabbit.

"Oh, quite sure," said Brer Fox. "You make me tired, asking that question over and over again. Stay here till I come back and I'll give you your share of the money."

He went off to market. He stood there and offered the spoons and forks for sale, the nice white towels, the new kettle, and the six pots of jam.

He wasn't long in selling them for he didn't ask very high prices. Soon he had ten shillings in his pocket, and he hurried back to Brer Rabbit.

"Look here!" he said. "Ten shillings between us! Five for you and five shillings for me."

"Thanks very much indeed," said Brer Rabbit, putting his money into his pocket. "I'll walk home with you, Brer Fox."

So the two of them walked back to Brer Fox's house together—and, of course, as soon as Brer Fox got indoors, he saw that six pots of jam had gone from his larder, that his kettle and spoons and forks were missing, and that there were no nice white towels in his cupboard.

"Hi-yi!" he yelled in a temper. "Someone's been here and taken my things! Wait till I catch the thief! Just wait! What else has he stolen? Oh, the scamp! Oh, the robber!"

"What has been stolen?" asked Brer Rabbit, keeping the other side of the gate. "How strange, Brer Fox—just the very things you sold at the market this morning! Now don't you think that's really VERY queer!"

Brer Fox turned and stared at Brer Rabbit, who was grinning all over his whiskery face! Brer Fox went quite green. He spoke to Brer Rabbit in a shaking voice.

"Whose house did you go to for those things I sold at the market?"

"Why, yours," said Brer Rabbit. "You said it didn't matter whose house I went to. Didn't you mean what you said, Brer Fox?"

Brer Fox gave such a dreadful yell that Brer Rabbit thought it was time to run, and run he did! My, how he ran! But when he got to the top of the hill he stopped and turned round.

"Brer Fox!" he called. "Are you still sure it wasn't stealing?"

And old Brer Fox hadn't anything to say to that!

36

Brer Rabbit and Mr. Lion's Tail

ONCE Brer Fox, Brer Wolf and Brer Bear made up their minds that they weren't going to put up with Brer Rabbit any longer.

"He's always plaguing us with his tricks and his bad ways," said Brer Wolf. "We'll go to his house this afternoon, and we'll haul him out and tell him what we think of him. Then we'll give him five minutes to say goodbye to his wife and children, and we'll take him off to cook him for our dinner."

"And a skinny mouthful he'll be," said Brer Bear.

"Never mind that," said Brer Fox. "Skinny or not, he'll be better in our pots than wandering loose in the woods, cheeking everyone he meets."

So that afternoon they went along to Brer Rabbit's house. But Brer Terrapin had warned him that they were coming.

"You take your old woman and your children and go," said Brer Terrapin. "I tell you, Brer Rabbit, when old Brer Wolf gets to planning with the others, things look bad for you. His head's full of brains."

"I'm staying here," said Brer Rabbit. "And you're going to do something for me, Brer Terrapin."

"What's that?" asked Brer Terrapin in alarm.

"Don't look so scary!" said Brer Rabbit. "All you've got to do is to stand by that bush there, and when you see Brer Wolf and Brer Fox and Brer Bear coming along, you're to squeal out: 'You be careful, all of you!

Mister Lion's just gone along here, roaring mad! You be careful!' "

"Oh, I can do that all right," said Brer Terrapin. "But why am I to shout that out, Brer Rabbit? It doesn't make any kind of sense to me."

"You'll soon see why," said Brer Rabbit. "And you come in this evening, Brer Terrapin, and we'll have supper in my house and a bit of a sing-song."

Brer Terrapin was surprised. He went and stood himself by the bush to wait for Brer Fox, Brer Wolf and Brer Bear to come by.

Brer Rabbit got busy. He took a thick piece of rope and undid the strands at the end, so that it looked like the tip of a lion's tufted tail. Then he climbed up on to his roof. He stuffed the rope down the chimney, and left the tufted end hanging out of it. Then down he went to the ground and ran into his house.

The other end of the rope was hanging down the chimney. He tied it to an iron staple in the fireplace. Then he set all his children in a row and taught them to open their mouths wide and bellow as loudly as they could, all together.

"That's good," said Brer Rabbit, at last. "I never did think to hear ten Rabbits roaring like one lion, but you make it sound easy! Now you sit in a row by the wall and wait till I give you the word to roar again, all together, with a one-two-three!"

Brer Terrapin was waiting patiently by the bush. He was most astonished to see what looked like a lion's tufted tail hanging out of Brer Rabbit's chimney. He stared at it for a long time. What was Brer Rabbit up to now?

Presently along came Brer Wolf, Brer Fox and Brer Bear. They looked very fierce and grim. Look out, Brer Rabbit, your enemies are here!

They saw Brer Terrapin standing by the bush. He put on a very frightened look. "Hey, look out there! You be careful, all of you! Mister Lion has just gone along here roaring mad! You be careful."

They all stopped. "What's Mister Lion roaring mad about?" asked Brer Fox looking frightened.

"I guess he's roaring mad with Brer Rabbit," said Brer Terrapin. "That's about it. Roaring mad!"

"We'd better get along to Brer Rabbit's house then," said Brer Wolf to the others. "If Mister Lion pounces on Brer Rabbit there won't be much of him left for our cook-pot!"

So they hurried along to the house. Brer Rabbit was watching out for them. He turned to the row of young rabbits. "Now ROAR!"

And roar they did, ten little roars that made one mighty big one. Brer Fox, Brer Bear and Brer Wolf stopped in a hurry.

"Did you hear that?" said Brer Wolf. "He's certainly roaring mad. Look—there's Brer Rabbit. Now we'll all pounce on him at once!"

But Brer Rabbit ran towards them, shouting loudly. "Come and help, come and help! I've got Mister Lion down my chimney!"

Brer Wolf suddenly saw the tail hanging out of Brer Rabbit's chimney. He gaped in surprise. He was quite sure it was Mister Lion's own tail. The others looked at it, too. The ten little rabbits gave another might roar.

"What's happened?" asked Brer Wolf at last.

"Well, Mister Lion came along here, roaring mad to get at me," said Brer Rabbit. "He was leaping about, and he leapt so high he went down my chimney. And there he's stuck, and I can't get him out."

The little rabbits bellowed all together, and Brer Wolf turned pale. "We'd better help him," he said at last.

"Yes, you come and help," said Brer Rabbit. "You take my ladder and get up on my roof and hang on to his tail. And when I say 'PULL' you all pull—maybe Mr. Lion will come up the same way as he went down. I'll go in and comfort him. He'll like to know his three friends are here."

Brer Rabbit ran indoors. Immediately a loud roar sounded again. Brer

Wolf ran to get the ladder. In a trice all three were up on the roof.

They took hold of what they thought was Mister Lion's tail and held on tightly. Brer Rabbit's voice came up the chimney. "Are you all ready? Then PULL!"

And pull they did! My how they pulled! Down below Brer Rabbit took out his knife and neatly cut the rope halfway up the chimney.

Things happened quickly after that. Brer Wolf, Brer Fox and Brer Bear felt themselves rolling down the roof, with the tail loose in their hands. They missed the ladder altogether and landed with a tremendous thud on the flower-beds below. They lay there, shaken to bits.

A tremendous roar came from the cottage. Brer Rabbit ran out, looking frightened. "You pulled his tail off, you turnip-heads! He's sitting down there in my kitchen, without a tail. My word, you wait until he comes out and catches you all!"

Well, they didn't wait. Brer Fox, Brer Wolf, and Brer Bear set off home as if a hundred lions were after them, not one. And they didn't go near Brer Rabbit's house for a long time after that.

Brer Terrapin spent a very merry evening with Brer Rabbit, and all the little rabbits were allowed to stay up for a sing-song because they roared so well. As for Brer Rabbit, he kept bursting out laughing every minute, and Brer Terrapin had to try and stop laughing in case he cracked his shell.

And what a surprise Brer Bear, Brer Wolf and Brer Fox are going to get when they next meet Mister Lion. He'll still be wearing his tail after all! What a rogue and a rascal Brer Rabbit is!

Brer Rabbit and The Glue

ONCE BRER RABBIT had a job to do in his garden. Some little bits of his fence had broken, and he guessed he would stick them with glue. So he put the glue-pot on the fire, stirred it up, and when it had melted he took it into the garden. He gathered together the bits of wood that wanted sticking, and began.

He was so busy that he didn't notice Brer Fox coming up behind him. It was only when Brer Fox pounced on him that he knew Brer Fox was there.

"Got you!" cried Brer Fox.

"Now, Brer Fox, please let me go," said Brer Rabbit in a calm sort of voice. "Can't you see I'm very busy?"

"What's the matter?" said Brer Fox, still holding tightly to Brer Rabbit. "I shall be busy soon too—having you for my dinner!"

"Oh, Brer Fox, don't be mean," said Brer Rabbit. "Just let me finish this job, for goodness' sake! I promised I would do it today, and I always like to keep my promises."

"What are you doing?" asked Brer Fox, gazing round at the glue-brushes, the glue-pot, and the wood.

"I'm mending this fence with glue," said Brer Rabbit. "Now don't ask if you can help, Brer Fox, because you couldn't. It's too tricky a job."

"What do you mean—too tricky for me?" said Brer Fox crossly. "You're not trying to make out that you are cleverer than I am, are you?"

"Oh no, not at all," said Brer Rabbit, dipping his brush in the glue. "It's only that I think you would make a mess of it."

Brer Fox glared at Brer Rabbit, who was now peacefully painting a board with strong glue. "Look here, Brer Rabbit," he began.

"Can't. I'm busy," answered Brer Rabbit. "Let me finish this job and I'll come with you, Brer Fox. But for goodness' sake don't interfere. I don't want everything spoilt."

Of course that made Brer Fox snatch up a big glue-brush and start work at once. "Hoo! I'll show you that I can glue things just as well as you can," he growled.

Brer Rabbit noticed that Brer Fox's tail was brushing against the garden-gate behind them. He grinned to himself. He put down his glue-brush and picked up the piece of wood he was working on to see if it was nicely done. When he set to work again, he didn't pick up his glue-brush—no, he took Brer Fox's tail, and dipped that into the glue-pot instead!

Brer Fox was angry. "Hey, you cuckoo! That's my tail!"

"Sorry," said Brer Rabbit. "It's so like a brush, Brer Fox. Sorry, sorry!"

Brer Fox took his tail out of the glue-pot and arranged it behind him again. It touched the gate as before. And pretty soon it stuck hard to the gate. Brer Rabbit watched out of the corner of his eye and grinned.

"I'll just go and get some more glue," he said to Brer Fox after a while, and he got up. Brer Fox got up to go with him, for he wasn't going to let Brer Rabbit go out of his sight, now that he had caught him so neatly. But something held him by the tail.

Brer Fox swung round angrily—and saw that his tail was stuck fast to the gate. "My tail's stuck!" he cried. "Brer Rabbit, you did it on purpose! Unstick it at once."

"What—and let you pounce on me again!" grinned Brer Rabbit. "I'm not such a silly as you think. You can stay there all day, if you like."

"I shall *not*!" yelled Brer Fox, and he tugged at his tail. Then he groaned deeply, for it hurt him very much. He sat and scowled at Brer Rabbit, who stood just out of reach, swinging the glue-pot.

"I'll get you a pair of scissors and you can cut your tail off," said Brer Rabbit kindly.

"Don't be silly," said Brer Fox, groaning again.

"There's no pleasing you," said Brer Rabbit. "So goodbye. I'll be back again soon to see how your tail is getting on."

Brer Rabbit went indoors, and watched from the window. He knew Brer Wolf was coming along that way soon—and sure enough he soon came ambling by. He pushed open Brer Rabbit's gate to see if Brer Rabbit was anywhere about, and he nearly knocked over Brer Fox, who was just the other side of it, his tail still stuck tightly to the gate.

"Hie! Be careful!" yelled Brer Fox.

"Heyo, Brer Fox," said Brer Wolf in surprise. "What are you doing?"

"I'm stuck!" said Brer Fox.

"What do you mean, 'stuck'?" said Brer Wolf in still greater surprise.

"Don't you know what 'stuck' means?" said Brer Fox snappily. "My tail's stuck to the gate. That tiresome Brer Rabbit did it. Now he offered

50

me a pair of scissors to cut off my tail."

"Well, that's what you'll have to do, isn't it?" said Brer Wolf, looking at the stuck-fast tail. "You'll have to stay here all night if you don't."

"Now do you think I'm going to cut off my beautiful tail?" demanded Brer Fox. "You must be mad!"

"Well, what else is there to do?" said Brer Wolf.

"I don't know," said Brer Fox sulkily.

"Ah—*I* know!" cried Brer Wolf. "I can take the gate off! Then you can go home, carrying the gate, can't you?"

"Well—it sounds silly, but perhaps it's the best thing to do," said Brer Fox gloomily. "Brer Rabbit will lose his gate then—and serve him right!"

Brer Fox heaved at the gate until it came off its hinges. Then Brer Fox took it on his back, with his tail still tightly stuck to it, and walked slowly off home, groaning all the way because of the weight of the gate and the pain in his tail. When he got home he asked Brer Wolf to get a great bath of hot water. When it was ready, Brer Fox sat beside it, with his tail and gate in the water, hoping to soak off the glue.

It came off after twelve hours' soaking, and poor Brer Fox got such a cold in his tail that he had to wear a handkerchief round it for three days to keep his tail from sneezing itself off.

He chopped up Brer Rabbit's gate and burnt it, and the next day found to his great rage that his own gate was gone—and there it was swinging gaily in Brer Rabbit's gateway.

"You just wait, Brer Rabbit, you just wait," he yelled.

"Righto!" yelled back Brer Rabbit. "I don't know what you want me to wait for, Brer Fox, but I'll certainly wait. Oh yes, I'll wait all right!"

So he's waiting—and Brer Fox's gate is still swinging merrily in Brer Rabbit's front gate. It *is* so annoying for Brer Fox!

Brer Bear's Red Carrots

ONCE Brer Bear had a whole field of fat red carrots. They grew there in hundreds, with their feathery green tops nodding in the breeze. Brer Rabbit thought they looked marvellous.

Now Brer Rabbit had just turned over a new leaf that week, and he felt it would be wrong to go and help himself to Brer Bear's carrots. "I must give people a chance to be kind," he said to himself. "I'll go and tell Brer Bear that I've turned over a new leaf and that I just can't let myself dig up any of his carrots without asking—and maybe he'll give me a whole lot."

So off he went to Brer Bear. Brer Bear was sitting in his front porch, basking in the sun. He wasn't very pleased to see Brer Rabbit, because he kept remembering the tricks that Brer Rabbit had played him.

"Good morning, Brer Bear," said Brer Rabbit politely. "It's a nice day, isn't it?"

"None the nicer for seeing *you*!" growled Brer Bear.

"Oh, Brer Bear! That's not a kind way to talk," said Brer Rabbit, shocked. "Why, I came to tell you that I'd turned over a new leaf!"

"About time too," said Brer Bear.

"You've a fine field of carrots," said Brer Rabbit. Brer Bear looked up at once.

"Oho! So it's my carrots you've come about," he said. "I didn't quite believe that new leaf idea of yours, Brer Rabbit."

"Well, that's just where you are wrong," said Brer Rabbit, trying to keep his temper. "I came to tell you that if I hadn't turned over a new leaf I'd have gone and dug up your carrots without asking you, to make myself some soup, but as I've made up my mind to be better in future, I came to ask you if I might have a few carrots. You can spare a few, surely?"

"Not to you Brer Rabbit, not to you," said Brer Bear. "And what's more, you can't make me give you any, no matter how many new leaves you turn over! No—once a scamp, always a scamp, is what I say, and I'm not giving any carrots to you at all."

Brer Rabbit stamped away in a rage. What was the use of turning over a new leaf if he couldn't get what he wanted? No use at all! All right—he would show Brer Bear that he would *have* to give him some carrots. Yes, he'd show him!

That night Brer Rabbit took his spade and went to Brer Bear's field. He dug up a whole sackful of fine red carrots. My, they were fat and juicy! But Brer Rabbit didn't eat a single one. No—he wasn't going to do that until Brer Bear had given him some.

He hid the sack of carrots under a bush and went home. Next morning he was up bright and early and went to the bush. He dragged the sack out and took it away down the lane not far from Brer Bear's house. It was very heavy indeed. Brer Rabbit puffed and panted as he dragged it along.

He waited until he saw Brer Bear coming down the lane for his morning walk. Then he set to work to drag the sack again, puffing as if he were a train going uphill! He pretended not to see Brer Bear, and

Brer Bear was mighty astonished to see Brer Rabbit dragging such a heavy sack down the lane.

"Heyo, Brer Rabbit," he said. "You seem to be too weak to take that sack along."

"Oh, Brer Bear, I've done such a foolish thing!" panted Brer Rabbit. "I've got such a lot of carrots to put in my store that I can't take them home! I shall have to leave them all here in the lane! Oh, why didn't you give me just a few when I asked you yesterday! Now all these will go to waste, for I'll have to leave them under a bush. I can't possibly drag the sack any farther."

Brer Bear didn't think for a moment that they could be *his* carrots. He opened the neck of the sack and looked inside. Yes, there were fine fat carrots there all right. He supposed that Brer Rabbit must have gone to market and bought them.

"You can't waste carrots," said Brer Bear. "It would be wrong."

"I know that," said Brer Rabbit. "But what am I to do?"

"I'll have them myself, if you like to take a few jars of honey in exchange for them," said Brer Bear, thinking that if he took the sackful it would save him the trouble of digging his own carrots that day.

"Oh, Brer Bear! How *kind* of you!" said Brer Rabbit, rubbing his whiskers in delight. "I thought yesterday that you were rude and unkind, Brer Bear. But today you are quite different. You are good and kind and generous. I like you."

Brer Bear couldn't help feeling pleased at this. He went into his house

and brought out three jars of honey. Brer Rabbit smelt them in delight.

"*Three* jars, Brer Bear! It's more than generous of you! How mistaken I was in you! I did so long for a few of your nice carrots yesterday, but this is almost better than carrots—though how I *do* long for carrot soup!"

"Well—you can have a few carrots out of this sackful if you like," said Brer Bear, still feeling very generous. "Here you are—one, two, three, four, five, six, seven, eight! Nice fat ones too!"

"Brer Bear, you're a mighty good friend!" said Brer Rabbit, stuffing the carrots into his big pockets and picking up the honey. "I meant to make you give me a few of your carrots—but I didn't hope that you would give me your honey too! Good-day—and thank you!"

Brer Rabbit skipped off as merry as a grasshopper in June. Brer Bear stared after him, scratching his head. Now what did Brer Rabbit mean by saying that he would *make* Brer Bear give him some of his own carrots?

And then Brer Bear suddenly had a dreadful thought and he hurried off to his field as fast as his clumsy legs would take him. There he saw where Brer Rabbit had dug up a whole sackful of carrots! And how poor Brer Bear stamped and raged!

"I've given him eight of my best carrots—and three pots of my best honey! Oh, the rascal–oh, the scamp! Turning over a leaf indeed! I'd like to turn *him* over and give him a spanking. And one of these days I will!"

But he hasn't yet! Brer Rabbit is much too clever to go near Brer Bear for a very long time.

Brer Rabbit Saves Brer Terrapin

ONE TIME Brer Fox was going down the big road and he saw old Brer Terrapin going to his home. Now Brer Fox knew Brer Terrapin was a good friend to Brer Rabbit, and it seemed to him it was a mighty good time to catch him. Brer Fox didn't have any kindly feelings towards people who were friends of Brer Rabbit.

Brer Fox ran back to his own house, which was not far off, and got a bag. Then he ran down the road again, rushed up behind Brer Terrapin, caught him up and threw him into the bag. He slung the bag across his back, then off he went, galloping home.

Brer Terrapin, he shouted, but it wasn't any good. He wriggled and struggled, but that wasn't any good either. Brer Fox just went on going, and there was old Brer Terrapin in the corner of the bag, and the bag tied up hard and fast.

But where was Brer Rabbit whilst all this was going on? Where was that long-eared, hoppetty-skippetty creature, that up-and-down-and-sailing round Brer Rabbit? He wasn't far off, you may be sure!

Brer Fox went trotting down the big road with the bag on his back—and Brer Rabbit was sitting in the bushes just by the side of the road. He saw Brer Fox trotting by and he saw the bag on his back too.

"Now what's Brer Fox got in that bag?" said Brer Rabbit to himself. "I don't know what it can be."

Well, Brer Rabbit sat in the bushes and wondered and wondered, but the more he wondered the less he could think what it was. He watched Brer Fox a-trotting down the road, and still he sat in the bushes and wondered.

"Huh!" said Brer Rabbit at last, "Brer Fox has no business to be trotting down the road carrying something other people don't know about. I guess I'll go after Brer Fox and find out what's in the bag!"

With that, Brer Rabbit set out. He hadn't got a bag to carry and he went mighty quickly. He took a short cut, and by the time Brer Fox got to his house Brer Rabbit had had time to get into his strawberry-bed and trample down a whole lot of plants. When he had done that, he sat down in some bushes where he could see Brer Fox coming home.

By and by Brer Fox came along with his bag across his back. He unlatched his door, he did, and then he threw Brer Terrapin down in a corner in the bag, and sat down to rest himself, for Brer Terrapin was mighty heavy to carry.

Brer Fox had hardly put a match to his pipe when Brer Rabbit stuck his head in at the door and shouted:

"Brer Fox! Oh, Brer Fox! You'd better take your stick and run out yonder. Coming along just now I heard a fuss going on in your garden, and I looked round and there were a whole lot of folk in your strawberry-bed, just a - trampling the strawberries down! I shouted at them, but they didn't take any notice of a little man like me. Make haste, Brer Fox, make haste! Get your stick and run. I'd go with you too, but I've got to get home. You'd better hurry, Brer Fox, if you want to save your strawberries. Run, Brer Fox, run! Hurry now."

With that Brer Rabbit darted back into the bushes, and Brer Fox dropped his pipe and grabbed his stick and rushed out to his strawberry-bed. And no sooner was he gone than old Brer Rabbit hopped out of the bushes and into the house.

He didn't make a bit of noise. He looked round and there was the bag in the corner. He caught hold of it and felt it to see what was inside. And suddenly something yelled:

"Ow! Go away! Let me alone! Turn me loose! Ow!"

Brer Rabbit jumped back astonished. Then before you could wink an eye he slapped himself on the leg and laughed out loud.

"If I'm not making a mistake, that's nobody's voice but old Brer Terrapin's!" said Brer Rabbit.

"Is that Brer Rabbit?" yelled Brer Terrapin.

"It is," said Brer Rabbit.

"Then hurry up and get me out," said Brer Terrapin. "There's dust in my throat, grit in my eyes, and I can hardly breathe. Get me out."

"Heyo, Brer Terrapin," said Brer Rabbit. "You're a lot smarter than I am—because here you are in a bag and I don't know how in the name of goodness you've tied yourself up in there, that I don't!"

Brer Terrapin tried to explain and Brer Rabbit kept on laughing, but all the same he untied the bag, took Brer Terrapin out and carried him outside the gate. Then, when he had done this, Brer Rabbit ran off to where he knew some wasps had a nest just about as big as a football.

The wasp-nest was in a hollow tree. Brer Rabbit slipped in at the bottom of the tree and there was the nest inside. He slapped his paw over the hole where the wasps went in and out, knocked the nest down into his bag, and there he had it, wasps and all!

Then back he raced to Brer Fox's house and flung the bag down on the floor, tied up fast. Well, the way he slammed that bag down on the floor stirred all those wasps up and put them into a very bad temper! They buzzed fit to make holes in the bag!

Soon Brer Rabbit saw Brer Fox coming down the back-garden, where he had been looking for the folks that had trodden down his strawberries. He had been putting the plants straight.

By the time Brer Fox got indoors Brer Rabbit was off and away into a bush and there he sat with Brer Terrapin, waiting to see what would happen.

Brer Fox went indoors, hitting the ground with his stick, and vowing that he would shake Brer Terrapin to bits, he was in such a bad temper.

He slammed the door and Brer Rabbit and Brer Terrapin waited. They listened, but at first they couldn't hear anything. By and by they heard the most tremendous noise!

"Seems like a whole crowd of cows running round and round inside Brer Fox's house," Brer Rabbit said to Brer Terrapin.

"I can hear chairs a-falling," said Brer Terrapin.

"I can hear the table turning over," said Brer Rabbit.

"I can hear the crockery smashing," said Brer Terrapin.

"Huh!" said Brer Rabbit, enjoying himself, "Brer Fox must be having a fine game with those wasps. What a surprise he got when he opened the bag to get you—and found a wasp's nest instead!"

Just as Brer Rabbit said that, Brer Fox's door flew wide open and out rushed Brer Fox, squalling and howling as if two hundred dogs had got him by the tail!

He ran straight to the river, he did, and plunged in to get rid of the wasps on him. Brer Rabbit and Brer Terrapin sat there in the bushes and laughed and laughed, till by and by Brer Rabbit rolled over and said:

"One more laugh, Brer Terrapin, and you'll have to carry me home!"

"Get on my back then, Brer Rabbit, get on my back," said Brer Terrapin. "I'll carry you all right. Shoo! That will teach Brer Fox not to go a-catching an old fellow like me and putting him into a dusty bag!"

Brer Fox came out of the river at last—but to this day he doesn't know how it was that though he put old Brer Terrapin into a bag, it was a nest of wasps that came out! And you may be sure Brer Rabbit never told him!

Brer Rabbit Raises the Dust

Now one time it happened that Brer Fox and Brer Rabbit, Brer Wolf, Brer Bear and the rest were always up at Miss Meadows'. When Miss Meadows had chicken for dinner in would come Brer Fox and Brer Possum, and when she had fried greens in would come Brer Rabbit. If she had honey it would be Brer Bear that would come popping his head round the door.

"I can't feed everyone," said Miss Meadows to the girls. "It's getting to be a real nuisance, having all the creatures pestering round. We shall have to do something to stop them."

Well, Miss Meadows and the girls, they thought what they could do to stop the animals coming so much. And they decided that the one that could knock most dust out of a rock, he should be the one that would still come to Miss Meadows' house. The rest must stay away.

So Miss Meadows told everyone that if they would come to her house the next Saturday evening, the whole crowd of them would go down the road to where there was a big flint rock. And each of them could take up the sledge-hammer and see how much dust he could raise out of the rock.

"I shall knock out a cloud of dust!" said Brer Fox.

"You won't be able to see for miles round when I get going with that sledge-hammer!" boasted old Brer Bear.

Well, they all talked mighty biggitty except Brer Rabbit. He crept

off to a cool place and there he sat down and puzzled out how he could raise dust out of a rock. He had never seen dust got out of a rock, and he guessed he never would. But he meant to do it somehow.

By and by, whilst he was a-sitting there, up he jumped and cracked his heels together and sang out:

"Brer Buzzard is clever, and so is Brer Fox,
But Brer Rabbit makes them all pull up their socks!"

And with that he set out for Brer Racoon's house and borrowed his slippers. When Saturday night came everyone was up at Miss Meadows' house. Miss Meadows and the girls were there; and Brer Racoon, Brer Fox, Brer Wolf, Brer Bear, Brer Possum and Brer Terrapin.

Brer Rabbit shuffled up late. By the time he got to the house, everyone had gone down the road to the rock. Brer Rabbit was waiting for that— and as soon as he knew no one was at home, he crept round to the ash-bin, and filled Brer Racoon's slippers full of ashes, and then he put them on his feet and marched off!

Brer Rabbit got to the rock after a while, and as soon as Miss Meadows and the girls saw him they began to giggle and laugh because of the great big old slippers he had on.

Brer Fox laughed too, and thought of something smart to say. "I guess old Brer Rabbit's got chilblains," he said. "He's getting old."

But Brer Rabbit winked his eye at everybody and said: "You know,

73

folks, I've been so used to riding on horseback, as these ladies know, that I'm getting sort of tender-footed when I walk."

Then Brer Fox, he remembered how Brer Rabbit had ridden him one day, and he didn't say another word more. Everybody began to giggle, and it looked as if they would never begin hammering on the rock. Brer Rabbit picked up the sledge-hammer as if he meant to have the first try. But Brer Fox shoved Brer Rabbit out of the way and took the sledge-hammer himself.

Everyone was to have three hits at the rock with the hammer, and the one that raised the most dust out of it was the one who would be allowed to go to Miss Meadows' house as often as he liked. All the others were to keep away from the house.

Well, old Brer Fox, he grabbed the hammer, he did, and he brought it down on the rock—*blim!* No dust came. Then he drew back the hammer and down he came again on the rock—*blam!* Still no dust came. Then he spat on his hands, gave a big swing and down came the hammer—*ker-blap!* and still not a speck of dust flew!

That was Brer Fox's turn finished. Then Brer Possum had a try, but he didn't raise any dust either. After that Brer Racoon took the hammer, and tried, but he couldn't make a speck of dust come at all. Then everyone else had a try except Brer Terrapin and Brer Rabbit, but nobody raised any dust at all.

"Now it's your turn, Brer Terrapin," said Brer Fox.

But Brer Terrapin, he said no. He had watched the mighty blows the others had given for nothing, and he wasn't going to tire himself out too.

"I've got a crick in my neck," he said. "I don't think I'll take my turn. Let Brer Rabbit have his. Looks like we'll none of us be able to raise any dust—so Miss Meadows and the girls won't have the pleasure of anybody's visit anymore!"

Brer Rabbit winked to himself, and grabbed hold of the sledge-hammer. He lifted it up into the air, and as he brought it down on the rock he jumped up and came down at the same time as the hammer—*pow!* And, of course, the ashes flew up out of his slippers and shot all round.

Brer Fox, he started sneezing away because the ashes got up his nose, and Miss Meadows and the girls began to cough and splutter.

Then Brer Rabbit lifted up the hammer again, jumped high into the air and landed with his feet and the hammer at the same time—*kerblam!*

"Stand further off, ladies!" he yelled "Here comes the dust!"

And sure enough the dust came, for the ashes flew again out of his slippers and everyone sneezed and choked and rubbed their eyes!

Then once more Brer Rabbit jumped up and cracked his heels together and brought the hammer down on the rock–*kerblam!* "Here comes the dust!" he yelled. And sure enough, the dust came!

Well, after that there wasn't much doubt about who should be the one to visit Miss Meadows and the girls, and Brer Rabbit went off arm-in-arm with two of the girls, grinning at all the others. They stood there, blowing their noses and glaring at Brer Rabbit; and Brer Fox, he took a sneezing fit and couldn't stop till the next morning.

Brer Racoon got his slippers back from Brer Rabbit all right, and nobody ever knew what Brer Rabbit had borrowed them for. Cunning old Brer Rabbit! There wasn't much he didn't know!

Brer Rabbit's Treasure

ONCE upon a time it got about that Brer Rabbit had a sack of treasure. "He keeps it in his shed," said Brer Fox to Brer Wolf. "I've peeked in the window and, sure enough, there's a sack full of something locked up in there."

"We'll go along each night and see if he has forgotten to lock the shed," said Brer Wolf. "It's certain that he didn't come by that treasure in any right way. We might just as well have it as old Brer Rabbit."

So each night, when it was dark, the pair of them went marching round to Brer Rabbit's shed. But each night the door was locked, and the pair of them didn't like to try and force the door in case Brer Rabbit heard them.

Old Brer Terrapin, who often liked to sleep in a hole near the shed, woke up each night when he heard Brer Fox and Brer Wolf creeping along. He poked out his skinny neck from under his shell, and listened to the pair whispering together.

"Oho!" said Brer Terrapin to himself. "So they're after Brer Rabbit's sack of treasure, are they? I must tell him."

He crawled off to tell Brer Rabbit. "You'd better be sure to keep that door locked," said Brer Terrapin. "Brer Fox and Brer Wolf come along each night hoping to get your sack of treasure."

Brer Rabbit grinned. "Is that so? Well, all I've got in my sack is carrots. Ho, they think it's treasure, do they, and they're after it! Well,

what about playing a little trick on them, Brer Terrapin?"

Brer Rabbit thought a bit and then he went off to market. He bought a whole lot of sponges, dry and sandy. He stuffed them tightly into a stout sack, and tied up the neck.

"Now, on the first wet night I'll leave the shed door unlocked," he said.

"And Brer Fox and Brer Wolf can pick up that sack. It'll give them a surprise long before they get home!"

The next night was stormy. Great black clouds poured down torrents of rain. Brer Rabbit wondered if Brer Fox and Brer Wolf would be along.

They came, holding umbrellas above their heads. Perhaps Brer Rabbit had forgotten to lock the shed this black, stormy night!

"He has!" whispered Brer Fox. "The door is open. Come on Brer Wolf—we'll soon get that sack of treasure!"

They felt about and came to the big sack of sponges. "Here's the sack," said Brer Fox. "I'll take my turn at carrying it first. My, it's not very heavy! That's queer."

"Hurry!" said Brer Wolf, thinking he heard a sound outside. "Maybe the treasure is paper money."

They went out into the night. Brer Rabbit and Brer Terrapin, who had been hiding under a nearby bush, followed the pair softly.

The rain poured down. Brer Fox couldn't use his umbrella as he was carrying the sack. It was soon soaking wet.

Then suddenly a weird voice rang out through the darkness, and Brer Fox almost dropped the sack in fright. The voice chanted a peculiar song:

"May the treasure break your back,
May your bones all creak and crack,
May you sink beneath the sack . . .
Bring it b-a-a-a-ack! Bring it ba-a-a-ack!"

"What's that?" whispered Brer Fox.

"Pooh! Only Brer Rabbit trying to frighten us into taking back the sack," said Brer Wolf. "Don't you know his voice? We're not going to take a scrap of notice."

They went on. The sponges in the sack began to get wet. They swelled up. They became heavier. Brer Fox began to pant.

"What's the matter?" said Brer Wolf. "That sack isn't heavy!"

"It's almost breaking my back!" panted Brer Fox. "You take a turn. It was so light to begin with."

Brer Wolf took the sack. He was most astonished at the unexpected weight. "My, it's heavy!" he said, and staggered along beneath it.

"Are your bones creaking and cracking?" asked Brer Fox, anxiously. "Oh, my goodness, I hope Brer Rabbit hasn't put a spell on this sack! You heard what he said about our backs breaking, and our bones cracking."

"And he said we'd sink beneath the sack!" groaned Brer Wolf, staggering along. The rain had now soaked all the sponges through and through, and they were very, very heavy. They were bursting to get out of the sack. They became heavier.

Brer Wolf almost sank beneath the sack. He panted to Brer Fox in alarm. "We'd better take it back, Brer Fox. You know what tricks Brer Rabbit can play. Better take it back before we come to any harm."

Brer Fox was alarmed. He agreed with Brer Wolf and the two of them turned back. They went right back to Brer Rabbit's shed and staggered in with the sack of sponges.

A lantern flashed on them. Brer Rabbit was behind them at the door. "Oho!" he said, grinning. "So you've taken my sponges for a walk and brought them back again. How kind of you!"

The swollen sponges could no longer find room in the sack. They burst it—and in front of Brer Fox and Brer Wolf, who stared at them in amazement, dozens of soaked sponges rolled on to the floor!

"Sponges!" said Brer Fox, in a hollow voice.

"Sponges!" said Brer Wolf. "No wonder they felt so light when we set out—and got so heavy when the rain soaked them. Brer Rabbit, this is a trick!" Brer Wolf was very angry.

"Serves you right," said Brer Rabbit. "You meant to play a trick on me and take my sack of treasure, didn't you? Well, that's it over there, see! You can't complain if I play a trick on *you*. And don't look as if you're going to eat me. I've got Mr. Dog to supper tonight, and he'll be after you if I give so much as a squeak!"

And with that Brer Rabbit went out of the shed, whistling. Brer Fox nudged Brer Wolf. "What about the real sack of treasure? Come on!"

They hauled away the sack Brer Rabbit had pointed to—and, my, that was heavy all right. Then away they fled in the darkness.

Brer Terrapin and Brer Rabbit rolled about on the ground, laughing till they nearly killed themselves.

As for Brer Fox and Brer Wolf, they hurried home in delight. But when they opened that sack, what do you suppose they found inside it? Why, nothing but old rotten potatoes! Brer Rabbit had tricked them again!

And the next time Brer Rabbit met them he held his nose with his paw. "Pooh!" he said, "you smell of rotten potatoes! Don't you come near *me*, Brer Fox and Brer Wolf!"

Brer Rabbit's a Rascal

Now, ONCE when Brer Rabbit was hard at work scraping the stones off his bit of ground, he heard a cry for help. Off he went, rake in hand, to see what the matter was.

It was the little girl belonging to the farmer. She had been fishing in the river and had slipped and fallen in. "Save me," she cried, and went swirling past Brer Rabbit, her skirt spreading out on the water.

Well, old Brer Rabbit he ran beside her, jabbing with his rake. And at last he got hold of the little girl's belt and hauled her to the bank. There she sat, sobbing and crying, her arms round Brer Rabbit's neck.

"You come home to your Ma," said Brer Rabbit. "You're wet. She'll dry you and give you a good hot drink."

So off they went together, the little girl clinging to Brer Rabbit as if she would never let him go. And my word, when the farmer heard how he had saved his little girl there wasn't anything he wouldn't have done for old good-hearted Brer Rabbit.

"There's a sack of carrots over there," he said. "Take it. And there's a sack of potatoes, too. You're welcome to it. And while you're about, help yourself to a sack of turnips. You're a born rascal, Brer Rabbit, but you're good-hearted, so you are! Now off you go while I still think good of you!"

Now, when Brer Rabbit was wheeling home his three sacks, whistling a merry song and feeling on top of the world, who should come along but

Brer Fox, Brer Bear and Brer Wolf. How they stared when they saw Brer Rabbit with so much food!

"Carrots! Turnips! Potatoes! Sacks of them!" said Brer Fox. "Hey, Brer Rabbit, give us some. And don't tell us you've come by them honestly, because we shan't believe you!"

Brer Rabbit was most annoyed. "You go and ask the farmer!" he said. "He gave me them with kind words, so he did!"

"Now you're telling stories," said Brer Wolf. "You give us some of those carrots and turnips and potatoes Brer Rabbit or we'll come along one night and help ourselves!"

"I *might* have given you some," said Brer Rabbit, wheeling his barrow away with his head in the air. "I *might* have given you some if you knew how to behave!"

Brer Bear, Brer Fox and Brer Wolf stared after Brer Rabbit. Brer Fox scratched his head. "Well, however he got those sacks he's going to share them with us, whether he wants to or not! Shall we go along to his place tonight and see where he's put the sacks?"

"Yes," said the other two, and Brer Fox grinned at them. "Meet me here. We'll slip along in the shadows—and my, won't Brer Rabbit be angry in the morning!"

Now, old Brer Rabbit had a kind of feeling that Brer Fox, Brer Wolf and Brer Bear might be along that night. He wheeled his sacks to his shed and emptied all the carrots, potatoes and turnips out on the ground. He picked out the bad ones and set them aside. Then he took a big broom and

swept all the roots along the ground to his cellar.

Bumpity-bumpity-bump—they rolled down into his cellar and he shut and locked the door. Then he went back to the shed again. He took the sacks to the pile of stones he had scraped off his ground and he filled them almost to the top with the stones. But right at the very top he didn't put the stones—he put a layer of bad carrots, a layer of poor potatoes, and in the third sack a layer of rotten turnips. Oh, Brer Rabbit, you're a wily one!

He dragged the sacks back to his shed and set them up against the walls. Then he went indoors, leaving the shed door unlocked.

"And if this isn't a nice easy way of getting rid of all those stones, well, I'll never know a better one!" said old Brer Rabbit.

Now, that night along crept Brer Fox, Brer Bear and Brer Wolf. There was a little moon so they kept well in the shadows. They came to the shed and tried the door. It wasn't locked—that was fine!

They slipped inside. Brer Bear pointed to the three sacks in glee. He looked in the top of one. He could see dimly in the moonlight—and he saw a layer of potatoes!

"Here are the potatoes," he said. "I'll take this sack. You follow with the others, Brer Wolf and Brer Fox."

They staggered out with the sacks. "My sack is mighty heavy!" said Brer Fox. "I never thought turnips could be such a dreadful weight."

"These carrots are heavy, too," panted Brer Wolf. "My, they must be good solid ones!"

Brer Rabbit saw the three of them through his window, staggering up

92

the lane in the shadows. He grinned to himself. "Nice of them to carry those tiresome stones!" he said. "I must thank them when I see them!"

Well, by the time Brer Fox, Brer Wolf and Brer Bear had reached their homes they couldn't walk a step farther! They sank down on the ground, panting. Brer Bear thought he would make some potato soup and he shook the sack hard—and out came six potatoes—and about twenty stones!

Then Brer Bear knew he had been tricked and he rushed to tell Brer Fox and Brer Wolf. But they had already found out, and dear me, the names they called old Brer Rabbit would have made his whiskers curl if he had heard them!

Brer Rabbit went out of his way to meet the three the next day. He raised his hat politely and gave his very best bow.

"My best thanks, gentlemen, for so kindly removing all those stones for me," he said. "I shall have another sackful tomorrow if one of you would like to call for it."

And then, my goodness me, he had to run for his life—but he didn't mind that because Brer Rabbit could always run faster than anyone else. As for Brer Bear, Brer Wolf and Brer Fox, they had to carry all the stones out of their gardens and empty them into the ditch. They were so stiff afterwards that they couldn't walk properly for days!

Ah, Brer Rabbit, it's hard to get the better of you, you rascal!

When Brer Rabbit Melted

"IT's hot!" said Brer Rabbit, panting, as he scampered through the wood. "Hotter than ever! I shall melt, I know I shall!"

He sat down under a big tree and fanned himself with a leaf. He puffed and he panted. He wished he could take off his warm fur coat, but he couldn't. He wished he could unbutton his ears and lay them aside, but he couldn't do that either.

"I must just go on being hot. But I shall melt," said Brer Rabbit. "I know I shall!"

"Then I'll come along and lick you up!" said a voice, and to Brer Rabbit's horror he saw Brer Fox peering round a tree at him. Brer Rabbit leapt to his feet at once.

He scurried off—but round another tree came Brer Bear, fat and heavy. He made a grab with his big paw at Brer Rabbit and knocked him flat. Before poor Brer Rabbit could get up, Brer Fox pounced on him and held him tight.

"Got you at last, Brer Rabbit!" said Brer Fox. "And I'll take you home with me and have you for supper tonight."

"Wait a bit!" said Brer Bear. "I was the one that knocked him down! I'll take him home to my wife for *my* supper!"

"Well, you won't," said Brer Fox. "I've been after Brer Rabbit for a very long time. If anyone is going to eat him, *I* am!"

"Now, you look here, Brer Fox," began Brer Bear, "you let me have my say. I'm going to eat Brer Rabbit, not you. My wife could do with a rabbit-pie. If anyone is going to eat him, *I* am!"

"Wouldn't she rather have a pot of new honey?" asked Brer Fox.

Brer Bear looked doubtful. He and his wife liked honey better than anything. But was this a little trick of Brer Fox's? He wasn't sure.

"I'll come home with you and help you to drag Brer Rabbit along," he said. "Then, if you show me the honey, I might say 'yes'."

"You let me go!" said Brer Rabbit, who was still underneath the paws of both Brer Bear and Brer Fox, and didn't like it a bit.

When they got to Brer Fox's house, they tied Brer Rabbit to a chair so that he couldn't move. Then Brer Fox and Brer Bear began to argue.

"You take my pot of honey and leave me Brer Rabbit," said Brer Fox, who didn't think there would be much pie left for him if Brer Bear shared his supper.

"Well, I don't think I will, till I know if Mrs. Bear wants me to," said Brer Bear, being very annoying.

"Well, go and ask her," said Brer Fox.

"Certainly not," said Brer Bear. "You'd eat Brer Rabbit up as soon as my back was turned! *You* go and ask her."

"Ho! And have you gobble up Brer Rabbit as soon as I was out of the house!" said Brer Fox. "No, thank you!"

"You let me go!" wailed Brer Rabbit, wriggling in the ropes that bound him to a chair.

The others took no notice of him. They glared angrily at one another. "Well, we'll leave Brer Rabbit tied up in this chair, and we'll lock the door, and I'll go to Mrs. Bear, whilst you sit *outside* the locked door," said Brer Fox, at last. "See, Brer Bear? I shall take the key in my pocket, so that you can't go in and eat up Brer Rabbit. He can't escape because he's all tied up. I'll be back as soon as I can to tell you what Mrs. Bear says."

As soon as Brer Rabbit was left alone he began to wriggle like mad. He managed to get his mouth down to one of the ropes, and he began to gnaw and gnaw.

Soon he gnawed right through the rope. It didn't take him long to get free then! He skipped to the windows. Alas, they were too heavy for him to open. He tried and he tried, but it was no good.

"*Now* what shall I do?" thought Brer Rabbit. "I haven't much time, Brer Fox will soon be back."

Then he grinned all over his whiskery face. He went back to his chair and tied up the ropes again. Then he hunted about for a soft broom, and pulled out a handful of hairs, which were very like his own whiskers. He scattered them on the chair seat.

He found some cotton wool, and put a round dob of it on the chair seat, too. It looked exactly like his white bobtail.

Then he noticed some roses in a bowl. He took them out and broke off their big, curved thorns. He put some of the thorns on the chair seat and some on the floor. They looked like claws!

He chuckled to himself and put the roses back into the bowl, without

thorns. Then he began to wail and howl.

"Oh, I'm so hot! Brer Bear, let me free. I tell you I'm melting!"

"You can't trick me like that, Brer Rabbit," said Brer Bear. "You're not melting! You just want to make me open this door and you'll jump out. But I shan't. Anyway, old Brer Fox has got the key."

Brer Rabbit went on howling. "I'm melting. Oh, my legs have melted! Oh, now my tail's melting! And there goes my body! I'll soon be melted completely if nobody helps me!"

Now, as soon as he heard Brer Fox coming back, Brer Rabbit shot into the coal-scuttle that stood near the door, pulled some bits of coal over himself, and lay quite still. He heard Brer Fox unlocking the door and talking to Brer Bear.

"Mrs. Bear says she'd rather have the honey. I'll get it and you can take it to her and leave Brer Rabbit with me."

"He's been howling and moaning all the time that he's melting with the heat," said Brer Bear. The door opened and the two walked in. They stopped at once when they saw the loose ropes and the empty chair.

"Where's he gone?" yelled Brer Fox, and darted to the door in case Brer Rabbit should appear from some hiding place and run out.

Brer Bear stared in alarm at the empty chair. He saw the long hairs there, like whiskers; he saw the white patch of wool, like a bobtail; and he saw the rose-thorns that looked exactly like claws.

"Brer Fox! He's melted! He said he was, and he has! Look—there's only his tail, his whiskers and his claws left! I tell you, Brer Fox, it's the end

of him—poor old Brer Rabbit has melted!"

Brer Fox came to see. He stared in amazement at the whiskers, the bobtail and claws. How could Brer Rabbit have melted like that? But it certainly looked as if he had!

"Yes, he's gone," said Brer Fox. "No rabbit-pie tonight. Well, good riddance to him. He was always tricking me, that rabbit. He won't trick me any more."

From the front gate came a cheeky voice: "Heyo, Brer Fox! Heyo Brer Bear! Isn't it hot? I do declare it's so hot that I'm melting!"

And there was that rascal of a Brer Rabbit laughing fit to kill himself. He had tricked old Brer Fox properly—and it wouldn't be long before he did it again—and again—*and* again!

Brer Fox's New House

IT HAPPENED once that old Brer Fox got himself a fine new house. My, wasn't he proud of it too! He called it Bushy Villa, after his tail, and he got Mrs. Bear to make him some blue curtains.

Now Brer Rabbit had wanted the house for himself, and he was in a great rage when he found that Brer Fox had walked in and taken it.

He set off to the house and knocked at the door, blim-blam!

"Who's there?" called Brer Fox.

"Brer Rabbit!" said Brer Rabbit.

"Come right in, Brer Rabbit!" sang out Brer Fox. But Brer Rabbit knew better than that. He just stood out there on the doorstep and shouted.

"Brer Fox! I'd like this house myself. I've come to offer you a good price for it."

"Then you can think again, Brer Rabbit," said Brer Fox, pleased to find that he had got something that Brer Rabbit wanted. "I'm in this house and here I stay! Good morning to you!"

Brer Rabbit was in a fine rage. He set off home, thinking with all his brains—and he had a good many. As he went along, head down and ears up, who should he meet but Brer Terrapin, the same old one-and-sixpence!

"How do, Brer Terrapin!" said Brer Rabbit, stopping and grinning at his old friend. "Why, Brer Terrapin, you are just the person I want to see. I've got a plan."

Brer Terrapin walked along by Brer Rabbit, listening to his plan of getting Brer Fox out of the house.

So it was arranged that Brer Terrapin should drop in at Brer Fox's house the next evening, and that Brer Rabbit should sit up on the roof with a fishing-line and drop things down on the end of the string.

"I'll tie my old tin teapot on first," giggled Brer Rabbit. "Then I'll tie an old boot. And then I'll tie Brer Fox's own hat. I'll slip into the hall and get it, once you are sitting talking to him, Brer Terrapin. That will give him a shock all right!"

Well, the next evening Brer Terrapin ambled along to Brer Fox's, and knocked at the door, blim, blam! Brer Fox was pleased to see him and asked him in.

"I've got a good fire, Brer Terrapin," he said. "Come along in and warm your toes."

As soon as they were safely in the parlour, Brer Rabbit crept into the hall and took Brer Fox's best hat. Then, with his old tin teapot under his arm, and a dirty old boot and his fishing-line in his pocket, he climbed quietly up to the roof. He sat beside the chimney and cocked his ear up to hear what Brer Terrapin was saying to Brer Fox.

"You know, Brer Fox," Brer Terrapin was saying, "this house feels kind of funny to me. I guess I wouldn't like to live in it myself!"

"Pooh!" said Brer Fox; "you don't know what you are talking about, Brer Terrapin. This house is just an ordinary, comfortable place, with nothing queer about it at all."

"There'll be something queer mighty soon!" said Brer Rabbit to himself, and he tied the tin teapot on to the end of his line. He dropped the line carefully down the chimney, and the teapot rattled against the bricks all the way down, clitter-clatter, clitter-clatter!

Brer Fox heard the noise and looked surprised. Brer Terrapin sucked at his old pipe and pretended to hear nothing at all. Down the chimney came the tin teapot and swung over the flames, just near Brer Fox's nose.

Brer Fox stared as if he couldn't believe his eyes. A teapot! Down the chimney! Hanging there! Now what could be the meaning of that?

He spoke to Brer Terrapin in a low voice. "Brer Terrapin! What do you suppose that tin teapot is doing in my chimney?"

Brer Terrapin turned and stared at Brer Fox as if he were greatly surprised. "Tin teapot!" he said. "What are you talking about, Brer Fox? Tin teapot, indeed! You'll be telling me it's dancing a jig next!"

Brer Rabbit, up on the roof, grinned when he heard that. He at once jerked his line and the teapot jumped up and down for all the world as if it were dancing a jig. Brer Fox clutched his whiskers and groaned.

"It *is* dancing a jig!" he said. "Brer Terrapin, do just look! Surely you can see a tin teapot dancing about in the chimney?"

Brer Terrapin turned towards the chimney and shut his eyes. "No," he said truthfully, "I can't see any teapot there, Brer Fox. Are you playing a joke on me?"

The teapot disappeared, and Brer Fox heaved a sigh. "Well, it's gone now," he said. "What a peculiar thing! A teapot in my chimney, and you don't see it, Brer Terrapin!"

"Don't you tell that kind of story to an old chap like me," said Brer Terrapin, settling himself more comfortably in his chair. "It's no good you expecting me to believe tales of teapots, Brer Fox!"

Slither-slither-slosh! Down the chimney came the old boot, tied tightly to the end of the string! Brer Fox leapt up from his chair in fright and stared at it.

"There's a boot now!" he cried. "Can't you see it, Brer Terrapin?"

"No, that I can't," said Brer Terrapin, looking at the chimney with his eyes shut again. "I can't see a thing. Do sit down, Brer Fox, and don't keep jumping and shouting. You make me quite uncomfortable."

The boot disappeared. Brer Fox stared at the chimney-place for a while and then sat down on the edge of his seat, watching the chimney. No sooner had he sat down than the boot slithered down again.

Brer Terrapin wanted to laugh but he dared not. "Goodness gracious, Brer Fox, what are you doing now?" he said. "Something else come down the chimney? Well, well, well, I don't know what you wanted to buy this house for! I heard that Brer Rabbit wanted it, and I'm sure I don't know why you didn't let him have it."

"I don't know why either," groaned Brer Fox. "I'd sell it to him now!"

Brer Rabbit grinned in delight. He tied the fine new hat on to the end of his line, and let that down the chimney too.

Brer Fox stared in horror. "Look, Brer Terrapin, look!" he said. "There's my new hat! Oh my, oh my, it's my new hat! I can't bear it!"

Brer Rabbit leant right over the chimney and nearly burst himself with laughing. But he didn't know what was going to happen next! Brer Fox was so wild at seeing his beautiful new hat dancing in the chimney covered with soot that he suddenly made a dart at it and caught hold of it! He pulled hard—and Brer Rabbit overbalanced and fell right into the chimney himself! Down he went, slither-swish, and landed in the hearth. He gave a great yell when he sat on the flames, and shot off like a bullet out of a gun!

Even Brer Terrapin got a shock that time, and he ran out of the house faster than any terrapin ran before. Brer Fox was scared too, for he wondered what was coming down the chimney *this* time! But when he saw it was Brer Rabbit, he was after him like lightning.

And Brer Rabbit lost a few hairs out of his tail that night, he was so nearly caught. He didn't get Brer Fox's house after all, and how he shook his fist when Brer Fox met him and called after him, "Hie ! Sweep! Would you like to come and do my chimneys for me?"

Aha, Brer Rabbit, you didn't win *that* time!

Brer Fox's Carrots

NOW ONE year it happened that Brer Fox had a mighty good crop of carrots. They were very fine, and Brer Fox was so afraid that Brer Rabbit would be after them that he made himself a little shelter of bracken leaves and slept there each night to guard his field.

So whenever old Brer Rabbit came sniffing along that way there was Brer Fox, his sharp ears cocked, and his sharp nose sticking out of the bracken shelter.

"Well, well," said Brer Rabbit to himself. "If I don't get my share of those carrots in the field, I'll wait till they're pulled! Maybe Brer Fox will hand me a few. He's got plenty."

So he watched and waited till he saw Brer Fox pulling his carrots. My, they were a fine juicy lot, and no mistake! Brer Rabbit watched from the hedge, and he longed and longed for a taste of those carrots.

"Heyo, Brer Rabbit!" said Brer Fox, with a grin. "I can see you a-sitting there, with your nose woffling like a mouse's! You can sit there all day if you like and watch the way I pull my carrots—but if you think you're going to nibble even the green tops of one, you'll have to think again!"

"Why, Brer Fox, you've so many that surely you can spare one or two for an old friend like me," said Brer Rabbit.

"Old friend! Old *enemy*, you mean!" said Brer Fox , with a snort.

"Now, listen to me, Brer Rabbit—you can make up your mind that

these carrots belong to *me*! And, what's more, I'm going to store them in my cellar and padlock the trap-door that leads to it! And if you can get any carrots out of a locked-up cellar, why you're very welcome!"

"Thanks, Brer Fox," said Brer Rabbit, seeming very grateful.

"Oh, you needn't thank me!" said Brer Fox.

"But you said I was welcome to any carrots I could get out of your

locked cellar," said Brer Rabbit. "And I was just thanking you for them."

"Then you're thanking me for nothing!" said Brer Fox, pulling up a great heap of carrots. "For nothing is what you'll get, my fine friend!"

Brer Rabbit grinned and disappeared. He ran off to Brer Fox's house, and sat in the garden and thought about that cellar. Then he hopped out of the garden and ran to a thick gorse bush a little way off on the common. There was a rabbit-hole there, and he popped down it.

Soon old Brer Rabbit was making a new burrow. The other rabbits came around and stared in surprise.

"Brer Rabbit! What's the excitement? You don't want to make a burrow near to Brer Fox's house! It's dangerous! When that fox is thin and hungry he may squeeze himself down a burrow and chase us!"

"You leave me to mind my own business," grinned Brer Rabbit, scraping away with his front feet, and sending showers of earth out with his back feet, so that the watching rabbits blinked their eyes and shook the dust out of their ears. Brer Rabbit said no more. He just went on burrowing and burrowing. He knew the way he was going all right—straight for Brer Fox's cellar!

All this time Brer Fox was pulling his carrots, and wheeling them to his house. He opened his trap-door and tipped the carrots down into his dark cellar. Then back he went again for another load of carrots. He went on until he had tipped every carrot down into his cellar. Then he wiped his hot forehead, took a drink of lemonade, and locked the padlock on his trap-door. He put the key into his pocket and buttoned it up.

"Well, if old Brer Rabbit can get my carrots now, he's cleverer than I think he is," said Brer Fox, and he got undressed and went to bed, for he was really very tired.

Now it didn't take Brer Rabbit very long to burrow right into Brer Fox's cellar. Pretty soon his head poked through a hole in the floor, and carrots began to fall into the burrow he had made. Brer Rabbit got his teeth into two or three, and mighty good they tasted! He stuffed as many as he could get into the basket he had brought with him, and scurried off home with them.

Then back he came with all his family, every one of them with baskets too, and, my goodness, what a hole they made in that cellarful of carrots! Soon Brer Rabbit's shed was over-flowing with red roots, and old Mrs. Rabbit was dancing a jig of joy to think of the carrot-soup they would have that winter.

"Old Brer Fox, he said I was welcome to any carrots I could get from his cellar," said Brer Rabbit truthfully to his wife. "So we might as well take what we can get, wife."

They didn't stop working until they had taken every single carrot—but just as they were filling the last basket one of the children giggled and woke Brer Fox. He heard a noise in his cellar, and he felt for his key at once.

Ah! There it was, safe in his pocket. Then what could that noise be in the cellar?

"My!" said Brer Fox suddenly. "I guess I know what it is! Old Brer Rabbit must have hopped down into my cellar just before I tipped my

carrots in! And he's sitting there now, nibbling them! Well, he'll be sorry in the morning, for I'll open the trap-door, jump down, and get him as sure as I've got whiskers! Rabbit-pie and carrots and parsley-sauce will be a nice supper tomorrow!"

Brer Fox got up and went to the trap-door. He didn't open it, but he rapped on it hard just to make Brer Rabbit sit up. "Heyo, Brer Rabbit!"

yelled Brer Fox. "I can hear you down there all right! You wait till tomorrow morning—I'll get you then, and you'll be sorry. Till then you're welcome to as many carrots as you like!"

Brer Rabbit grinned round at his family. Then he put on a very scared sort of voice, and answered Brer Fox.

"Mercy, Brer Fox, mercy! Let me go in the morning! Mercy!"

"Ha! You can just sit there all night and think of what's going to happen tomorrow!" said Brer Fox. He got back into bed and fell asleep.

Brer Rabbit and his family disappeared down the burrow—and then Brer Rabbit filled up the hole he had made into the cellar, and left everything neat and tidy. Back they all went, locked up their carrots, and tumbled into bed to fall asleep in half a minute!

In the morning Brer Fox went to unlock his cellar door, pleased to think he had caught Brer Rabbit at last! He went down a few steps and then shut the trap-door down, for he didn't mean Brer Rabbit to skip out of it.

But tails and whiskers! When poor Brer Fox looked into his cellar, what did he see? Nothing! Nothing at all! Not a carrot. Not a rabbit. It was quite empty.

Brer Fox couldn't believe his eyes! He sat on the steps and looked and looked, wondering if he was in a dream.

And then he heard a small noise above him, and he shot up the steps at once—but he was too late! Brer Rabbit had locked the trap-door with the key that Brer Fox had left on the floor nearby! Brer Fox was a prisoner!

"Brer Fox!" called Brer Rabbit. "I hope you'll enjoy your carrots!"

"Brer Rabbit, they're gone!" said Brer Fox, more puzzled than he had ever been in his life.

"Yes, I took them," said Brer Rabbit. "You said I was welcome to any I could take, didn't you now, Brer Fox?"

Then Brer Fox went quite mad with rage and banged on the trap-door as if he'd break it in two.

"Now, now!" said Brer Rabbit. "What a naughty temper! I'm just going, Brer Fox, so goodbye."

"You unlock me, Brer Rabbit!" shouted Brer Fox. "Do you want me to starve in here?"

But Brer Rabbit was gone with a hoppitty skip! Brer Fox was left in the dark cellar, puzzling and wondering how Brer Rabbit could have got there and taken all the carrots when the trap-door was locked.

And there he had to stay till the next day, when Brer Bear came calling and was mighty scared to hear Brer Fox wailing in the cellar! Brer Bear unlocked the trap-door, for Brer Rabbit had left the key, and out came Brer Fox, hungry and thirsty but so angry that he could neither eat nor drink. He wanted to rush off and catch Brer Rabbit at once, but Brer Bear calmed him down.

"Now, Brer Fox, don't be rash," he said. "If Brer Rabbit can play you such a trick as this, he's too mighty clever for you–so just you sit quiet and wait your time!"

And that's what poor Brer Fox did, whilst Brer Rabbit and his family feasted on carrot-soup and grew as fat as butter all the winter through!

Brer Rabbit is So Clever

Now once old Brer Rabbit had a fine store of jam in the barn, that Mrs. Rabbit had made. There wasn't room to put it in the larder, so Brer Rabbit made some shelves in his barn and put the jam there.

But old Brer Bear soon sniffed it out and he went one night to take some. He got in through the window and went off with seven pots of fine strawberry jam. Brer Rabbit was so angry next day when he found the seven pots missing.

"I'll catch Brer Bear and make him pay dearly for that jam!" said Brer Rabbit to himself. So he went off to find some straw, and put it down in the barn. Then he went to the holly tree and looked under it for some sharp-pointed fallen leaves.

Brer Rabbit mixed the sharp holly leaves in with the straw, grinning away to himself all the time. Now whoever came stealing at night would tread on a prickly leaf and get a shock!

Well, that night along came old Brer Bear for a few more pots of jam again. He climbed in through the window and went to the shelf of jam—and on the way he trod heavily on a sharp-pointed holly leaf! He let out a yell and hopped round in pain.

Brer Rabbit was outside, waiting. He opened the door and rushed in with a big stick. He pretended not to know that Brer Bear was there and he slashed about in the straw as if he was mad!

"I'll get that snake!" he shouted, as he slashed about. "I'll get that snake! It won't bite me if I know anything about it! I'll get that snake!"

Well, when Brer Bear heard Brer Rabbit shouting about a snake he got very frightened. Was it a snake that had bitten his foot? Oh my, oh my, he might be poisoned and die!

Brer Bear let out a groan and Brer Rabbit stopped slashing about and spoke as if he was mighty surprised.

"Who's there?" he asked.

"It's me—Brer Bear," said Brer Bear, lumbering over to Brer Rabbit in the darkness. "Oh, Brer Rabbit, I think that snake's bitten me!"

He trod on another holly leaf and let out such a yell that he made Brer Rabbit jump. "It's bitten me again!" he shouted. "It's bitten me again! Oh, Brer Rabbit, I'll die! I've been bitten by a poisonous snake in the straw."

"Well," said Brer Rabbit, most severely, "I should like to know what you are doing stamping in my straw at this time of night, Brer Bear."

"Oh, Brer Rabbit, if you must know, I was after your jam," groaned Brer Bear. "And now, please go and get a doctor. Do you want me to die of a snake-bite in your barn?"

"Well, it might serve you right," said Brer Rabbit, grinning away to himself in the dark, thinking of the holly leaves in the straw.

Brer Bear tried to get to the door, but unluckily he trod on yet another holly leaf. He gave such a yell that the windows shook!

"That snake's bitten me again! Oh, oh, what shall I do? Go fetch a doctor quickly, Brer Rabbit! You can have back your seven pots of jam!"

"And what else?" demanded Brer Rabbit.

"Oh, you can have seven pots of honey, too," wept Brer Bear.

"Anything else?" asked Brer Rabbit.

"Yes—you can have seven pots of chutney," groaned Brer Bear.

"Well, I'll go and get it all now," said Brer Rabbit. "Now you stay here, Brer Bear, because if you go stamping about the barn that snake is sure to bite you again!"

Off sped Brer Rabbit. He came to Brer Bear's house and got the jam, the honey, and the chutney. He tore back again and set it neatly on the shelf. Brer Bear was lying groaning in the straw, not daring to move.

"I think my legs are swelling up," he said ."I think I'm poisoned."

"Well, I'll put some wonderful snake-ointment on you," said Brer Rabbit, grinning away in the darkness. "It will soon make you right!"

Brer Rabbit, went into his house and got a tin of black boot-polish. He went to the barn with a lantern.

"Oh, Brer Rabbit, you are kind," said Brer Bear. "Just rub the ointment on and I can go to the doctor then. Rub it on quickly."

Brer Rabbit smeared black boot-polish all over Brer Bear's feet.

"There!" he said. "You will find that your feet won't hurt you at all tomorrow. This is wonderful for snake-bites."

So old Brer Rabbit rubbed more black boot-polish on, grinning away.

"Now, Brer Bear, you listen to me," he said. "As soon as you get home, lick off all this ointment and put a fresh lot on out of the tin. Don't forget, will you? If you do that, you won't need to go to the doctor."

"Oh, thank you, Brer Rabbit," said Brer Bear gratefully. He hobbled out of the barn, and did not tread on any more holly leaves! Off he went home, glad to find that his legs didn't hurt him at all.

So he sat down when he got home and began to lick off the black boot-polish. It tasted simply terrible. Brer Bear didn't know how he was going to lick it all off. He sat with his tongue hanging out, feeling mighty sick. Then he began again—but he just *had* to stop, for the taste was dreadful.

"I'll put the fresh ointment on top of the old," he said at last, and picked up the tin. On it he read: 'Black boot-polish!' Brer Bear stared as if he simply couldn't believe his eyes!

"*Boot*-polish! And I've been licking it! *Boot*-polish!" shouted Brer Bear, and he went to rinse out his mouth. But he couldn't get the black off!

And for two whole weeks, whenever Brer Rabbit met Brer Bear he shouted out, "How's your tongue, Brer Bear? How's your tongue? Let's have a look at your tongue!"

Didn't Brer Bear growl! He'd lost seven pots of honey and seven pots of chutney—and got his tongue well blacked! Poor Brer Bear—he won't go stealing from old Brer Rabbit again!